# Doodle Girl

To my beautiful niece Abi xxxx

SS

Dear Charlotte and Chloe, enjoy the magic.
Lots of love xxxx

LT

for My Stars

MM

SIMON AND SCHUSTER
First published in Great Britain in 2016 by Simon and Schuster UK Ltd
1st Floor, 222 Gray's Inn Road, London WC1X 8HB
A CBS Company

Text copyright © 2016 Suzanne Smith & Lindsay Taylor
Illustrations copyright © 2016 Marnie Maurri

The right of Suzanne Smith & Lindsay Taylor to be identified
as the authors and Marnie Maurri as the illustrator of this work
has been asserted by them in accordance with the
Copyright, Designs and Patents Act, 1988

A CIP catalogue record for this book is available from
the British Library upon request

ISBN: 978-1-4711-2318-4
eBook ISBN: 978-1-4711-2380-1

Printed in China
2 4 6 8 10 9 7 5 3 1

# Doodle Girl

## and the
## Monkey Mystery

by SUZANNE SMITH & LINDSAY TAYLOR

Illustrated by MARNIE MAURRI

SIMON AND SCHUSTER

LONDON    NEW YORK    SYDNEY    TORONTO    NEW DELHI

This is

# Doodle Girl.

She lives in a **BIG** RED SKETCHBOOK.
But it's not just **ANY** sketchbook.
It's a **MaGiC** sketchbook.

And Doodle Girl has a MAGIC PENCIL too.
Whenever she whispers the words
'Draw, draw, draw...'

AMAZING
ADVENTURES
begin to unfold.

All it takes is a doodle...

One day Doodle Girl was
taking a stroll with her
friends, when they
discovered

A

POINTY SHAPE

in the sketchbook.

"Doodling daydreams! Whatever could it be?"
said
Doodle Girl.

Mr Whizzy and Miss Ladybird
wanted to play.
Was it a **SEE-SAW**?

The Small Squeakies were SURE it was **CHEESE**.
It just HAD to be YUMMY,

scrummy

CHEESE!

But Doodle Girl had another idea . . .

"Draw, draw, draw," she whispered.

And with a D-A-S-H here, a DOT there and a squiggle of

her MaGiC PENCIL, the POINTY SHAPE soon became

something FABULOUS...

# A MAGNIFICENT AEROPLANE!

"Ja-daa!" said Doodle Girl. "Pop your goggles on everyone.

It's time for an adventure! Let's go!"

UP, UP, **UP** they soared, through the clouds and across the SHIMMERING ocean.

Liddle Birdie spotted something.

"Look! An island!"

"Hold on tight, this might get a bit bumpy!"

said Doodle Girl.
But it wasn't bumpy at all.

DOWN,
DOWN,
DOWN
they gently glided
until . . .

They landed
on a beach.
"Let's explore,"
said
Doodle Girl.

They followed a sandy path which

...led DEEPER and DEEPER into the cool JUNGLE until they reached . . .

OOOOOO!

HAROOOOOO!

HAROOOOOOOO!

"Whatever's that?" said Doodle Girl.

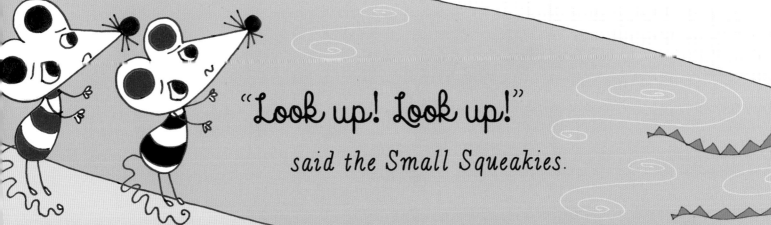

"Look up! Look up!" said the Small Squeakies.

It was a little monkey.
He was dangling
UPSIDE DOWN in a tree.

HAROOOOOO!

Below him were
TWO CROCODILES swimming in
slow circles and watching him closely.
VERY CLOSELY.

"He's stuck!" said Doodle Girl.
"We've got to help him!"
Suddenly there was a loud **CREAK!**
The branch was breaking . . .

But Doodle Girl knew just what to do.
Whispering to her MaGiC PENCIL,
"Draw, draw, draw,"
she *swirled*
a D-A-S-H here
and a

DOT there.

"Ta-daa!"

The little monkey bravely
let go of the branch.

# PLOMP!

He landed safely in
the spoon.

SQUELCH!

SQUASH!

But the crocodiles had crawled out of the swamp and were coming towards them.

Uh-oh!

So, with a quick "Draw, draw, draw", Doodle Girl whisked out her MaGiC PENCIL, and drew . . .

A GIANT ICE CREAM!

s **BLOB** after **BLOB** of yummy ♥ ice cream

flew into the mouths of
the **HUNGRY** crocodiles.

They soon had **FULL** tummies.

"What a snip-snappy tasty adventure!" laughed Doodle Girl.

And after an **AMAZING ICE CREAM PARTY**, it was time to go back to . . .

. . . the pages of the **BIG** RED SKETCHBOOK.

Doodle Girl looked at the **POINTY SHAPE**.

"Now I know what it's for," she said to herself.

And with
a final
"Draw, draw, draw",

she doodled
each of her friends
a perfect little paper aeroplane.

Happy doodling
everyone!

# THIS ANNUAL BELONGS TO...

HC
CB
HARPERCOLLINS
CHILDREN'S BOOKS

# CONTENTS

6    WELCOME TO MY ANNUAL

8    THE WORLD OF DAVID WALLIAMS MAP QUIZ

10    MEGAMONSTER'S MEGAMAZE

11    CREATE A STORY

12    HOW TO DRAW LIKE TONY ROSS

14    SPOT THE DIFFERENCE

16    ALL ABOUT THE WORLD'S WORST PETS

18    THE WORLD'S WORST PETS: SILLY SID'S SNAKE

24    WHICH DAVID WALLIAMS CHARACTER ARE YOU?

26    HOW TO MAKE SLIME

27    SLIME SEARCH

28    ALL ABOUT THE WORLD'S WORST MONSTERS

30    THE WORLD'S WORST MONSTERS: MUMMY THE MUMMY

36    HOW TO BLING YOUR GRANNY'S RIDE

38    COLOUR IN THAT FING

40 AUNTIE ALBERTA'S OWLEUM

42 ALL ABOUT CODE NAME BANANAS

43 GERTRUDE'S PARTY TRICKS

44 ALL ABOUT THE WORLD'S WORST CHILDREN

46 MEET THE BLUNDERS

47 UN-BLUNDER THESE BLUNDERS

48 COLOUR IN THE BLUNDERS

49 INVENTIONS WITH BERTIE

50 ALL ABOUT ASTROCHIMP

51 THE WORLD OF ASTROCHIMP

52 ASTROCHIMP

58 ALL ABOUT SPACEBOY

59 MAKE YOUR OWN SPACESUIT

60 CONSTELLATION STAR-TO-STAR

61 JOE SPUD'S CROSS-COUNTRY SLIDES AND LADDERS

62 LEONARD SPUD'S GUIDE TO LOO-ROLL MODELLING

64 FIND THE BLACK CAT

65 SHINY SPOT THE DIFFERENCE

66 THE MEGA QUIZ!

70 ANSWERS

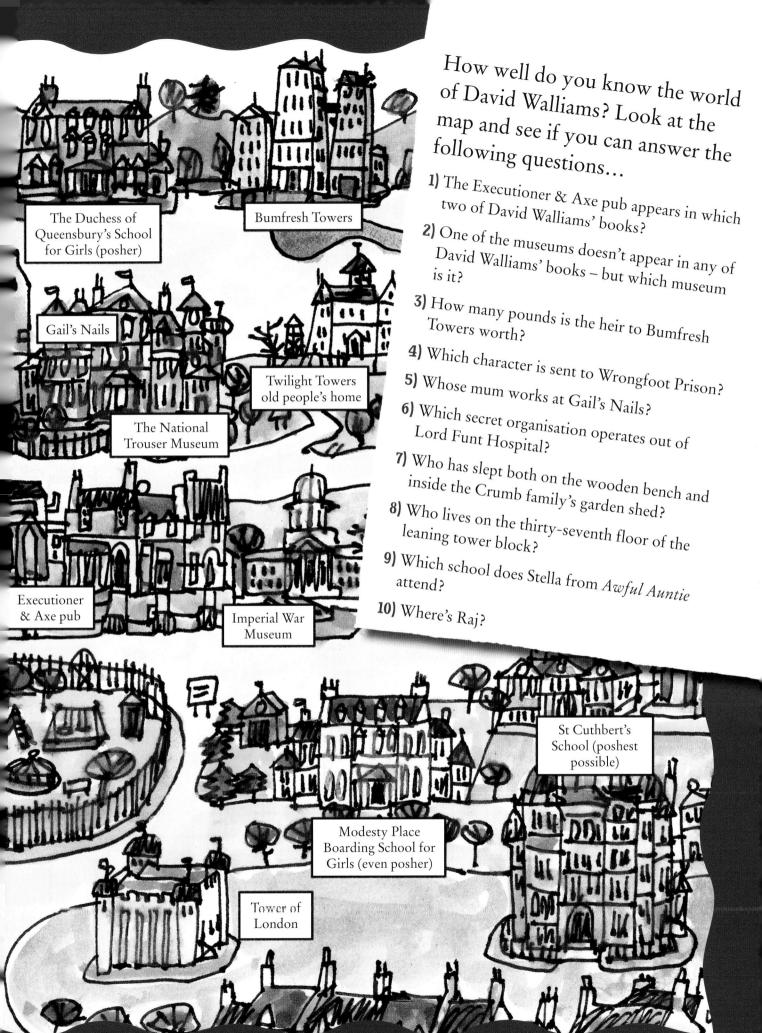

## How well do you know the world of David Walliams? Look at the map and see if you can answer the following questions...

**1)** The Executioner & Axe pub appears in which two of David Walliams' books?

**2)** One of the museums doesn't appear in any of David Walliams' books – but which museum is it?

**3)** How many pounds is the heir to Bumfresh Towers worth?

**4)** Which character is sent to Wrongfoot Prison?

**5)** Whose mum works at Gail's Nails?

**6)** Which secret organisation operates out of Lord Funt Hospital?

**7)** Who has slept both on the wooden bench and inside the Crumb family's garden shed?

**8)** Who lives on the thirty-seventh floor of the leaning tower block?

**9)** Which school does Stella from *Awful Auntie* attend?

**10)** Where's Raj?

Map labels:

- The Duchess of Queensbury's School for Girls (posher)
- Bumfresh Towers
- Gail's Nails
- Twilight Towers old people's home
- The National Trouser Museum
- Executioner & Axe pub
- Imperial War Museum
- St Cuthbert's School (poshest possible)
- Modesty Place Boarding School for Girls (even posher)
- Tower of London

**ANSWERS ON PAGE 70**

# MEGAMONSTER

# MEGAMONSTER'S MEGAMAZE

Welcome to the Cruel School, where the teachers are as monstrous as the school dinners.

HARUMPH...

Help Larker escape the Megamonster and reach her friend Spod!

SPOD, I'M ON MY WAY!

START

FINISH

**MONSTROUS FACT**
Larker was sent to The Cruel School for pulling a prank! People call her Larker because she's always larking about.

MEET THE SCHOOL'S BIGGEST KID, SPOD. HE MAY LOOK TOUGH, BUT HE WOULDN'T HURT A FLY!

ANSWER ON PAGE 70

# MEGAMONSTER
# CREATE A STORY

Use these prompts to plan your own monster-themed tale.
Your story could have the same characters and setting as
*Megamonster*, or you could make up your own!

1. .................... jumped out of bed ready for adventure.

2. They pulled back the curtains. The weather was ....................

3. When they looked up, they saw a gigantic monster that looked like ....................

4. Its name was ....................

5. The monster was covered in fur/scales/feathers/ ....................

6. It had plans to take over the world/gobble everyone up/ ....................

7. So .................... came up with a plan

WRITE YOUR HERO'S NAME HERE

8. The plan was .................... ....................

You have the makings of an exciting story here.
So, find some blank paper and get writing.

# ROBODOG

# SPOT THE DIFFERENCE

Can you find 8 differences between picture a and b?

a

b

## Woof!

Say hello to Robodog. This adventurous fellow is the latest recruit of the Police Dog School. Will he have what it takes to save Bedlam from destruction?

## The Lost Patrol

Meet the other members of Police Dog School. Scarper, Plank and Gristle. Let's just say they need all the help they can get.

Can you find 8 differences between picture c and d?

c

d

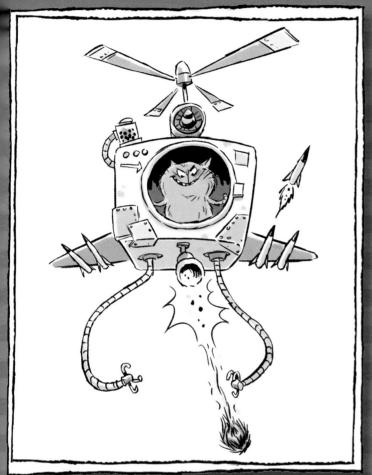

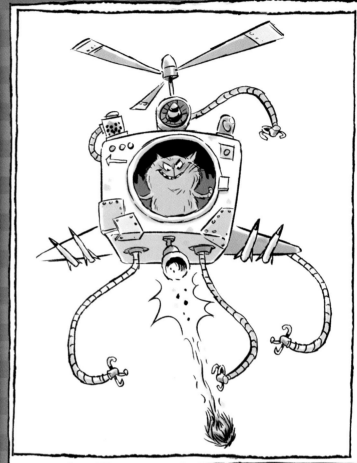

YOU COULD TRY COLOURING IN THE PICTURES TOO!

GRISTLE

SCARPER

PLANK

ANSWERS ON PAGE 70

# ALL ABOUT THE WORLD'S WORST PETS

Pets come in all shapes and sizes – and all shades of terrible.
From a thieving budgie to a blood-curdling bear, these animals
definitely deserve their title as the world's worst pets!

## PICASSO THE PONY

PICASSO IS THE PRETTIEST PONY AROUND – THAT IS UNTIL SPOILT KID MOLLY CODDLE RUINED HIS COAT WITH PAINT. NOW HE'S READY TO 'STIRRUP' TROUBLE AND GET HIS REVENGE.

## MONTY THE MUSICAL DOG

## HOUDINI THE BAD BUNNY

THIS BUNNY WISHES SHE BELONGED TO THE MOST FAMOUS MAGICIAN OF ALL TIME. INSTEAD, SHE BELONGS TO THE WORST – THE GREAT FIASCO.

## CANDELABRA THE SUPERVILLAIN'S CAT

## HARTLEY THE HAMSTER AND GERALD THE GERBIL

## FURP THE FISH

THIS POCKET-SIZED PAIR DISAGREE ABOUT EVERYTHING, ESPECIALLY WHO THEIR OWNER BETSY LOVES MORE.

## GRISELDA THE GRIZZLY BEAR

## SILLY SID'S SNAKE FIDO

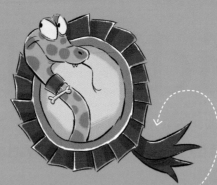

SILLY SID IS ONE SILLY SAUSAGE. WHO ELSE COULD BUY A SNAKE AT A PUB AND MISTAKE IT FOR A PUPPY!

## BUMBLE THE BURGLING BUDGIE

# NOW IT'S YOUR TURN!

How does your pet compare to the ones in this book? Write about them, and why they are the world's best or worst. Then draw your very own pet portrait.

THE WORLD'S BEST PET

IS YOUR PET **BIG** OR SMALL?

ARE THEY FAST OR SLOW?

HOW HAIRY ARE THEY?

MEET DAVID'S DOGS, BERT & ERNIE!

## THE WORLD'S WORST PETS

# Silly Sid's SNAKE

What happens when you cross a snake and a very silly man? Find out in this *hiss*-terical tale that is sure to make you howl with laughter...

Snakes slither to the top on a list of the world's worst pets. They are joint world's worst with spiders (creepy AND crawly), bats (all that blood-sucking nonsense), sharks (like to eat children), hippopotamuses (take up too much space) and worms (not much **conversation**). So, what would happen if one of your parents brought home a snake?

That is what Silly Sid did.

"Kids! Look what I bought you down the pub!" announced Silly Sid as he burst through the door of the family home. Silly Sid was wearing his usual mismatched colours and patterns. His hair was a wild bush, his glasses were on all wonky and he had his right shoe on his left foot and his left shoe on his right. Well, Silly Sid was rather silly, as his name suggests. Over his shoulder, he was carrying a large cloth sack. Something was wriggling and Wraggling* and wruggling** around inside it.

Silly Sid's three not-at-all-silly kids stopped playing Snakes and Ladders, and rushed over excitedly to greet him. Like most children, they had wanted a pet for as long as they could remember.

"Is it a kitten?"

"Is it a bunny?"

"WHOA! WHOA! WHOA!" exclaimed their dad. "Just wait and see!"

With that, he reached into his bag and pulled out a...

\* Wraggling means wruggling.
\*\* Wruggling means wraggling. See your *Walliamsictionary*.

# SNAKE! "HISS!"

Not just any snake – one of the **biggest** species of snake in the world… A PYTHON! The snake stuck out its tongue, then, with what looked like a smile, wrapped itself round Silly Sid… and began to squeeze!

"ARGH!"

"HELP!" screamed the children.

"What's all this noise?" cried Mum as she stormed into the living room with her hair in curlers.

Mum's name was Nancy. Nancy had been married to Silly Sid for twenty long, silly years. She thought she'd seen it all before, but this time Silly Sid had done something sillier than ever!

"Oh no, Silly Sid, what on earth have you done now?" cried Nancy on seeing the snake.

Immediately, she tried to yank the python off her husband. Any moment now, it was going to squeeze the life out of him.

"HISS!"

"What do you mean?" he asked innocently as the snake wrapped itself round his neck. Silly Sid didn't know he was silly, which added an extra layer of silliness.

Silly Sid's life had been one long list of silly mistakes: SILLY SID'S SLIP-UPS!

However, of all Silly Sid's mistakes, bringing home a PYTHON was by far the silliest.

"The kids wanted a pet!" protested Silly Sid.

"Not one like that, you silly, silly man!" snapped Nancy as she just managed to pull the python off him.

"HISS!"

The **huge** snake slithered along the floor, and the kids leaped behind the sofa.

"HISS!"

All three children were called Bob. Bob, Bob and not forgetting Bob. Silly Sid named all his children Bob so that he wouldn't forget what they were called. Even though one of them was a girl. He tried to call his wife Bob too, but Nancy was having none of it!

"NOOO!" screamed Bob.

"PLEASE!" yelled the other Bob.

"I AM S-S-S-SCARED!" cried out the girl Bob.

Nancy yelled at her husband, "Silly Sid! The Bobs wanted something cute and cuddly, like a puppy!"

"This is a puppy!" stated Silly Sid with a smile.

"That is NOT a puppy, you silly, silly, silly man!" shouted Nancy.

"The bloke in the pub, Mr Shifty, who flogged it to me, swore it was!" replied Silly Sid.

"Well, that Mr Shifty saw you coming! You seriously believed him?"

The snake was now dangling **upside down** from the lightshade.

"*HISS!*" it hissed, as it swung from side to side in obvious delight at its new playground. This was so much better than being in a sack!

"Yeah! And it was a bargain. 'Last puppy in the litter,' he said. Only a hundred quid."

"A HUNDRED QUID!" exclaimed Nancy. "I GIVE UP!"

"I'm not stupid. I asked Mr Shifty why the puppy was so big. And he told me it was a fully grown puppy."

"Dad! A fully grown puppy would be a dog," chipped in one of the Bobs.

The snake slithered on to Nancy's shoulder and began wrapping itself round her!

"*HISS!*" hissed the snake, its eyes glowing with glee at the **TERROR** it was causing.

"C-C-CRIPES!" cried Nancy, her teeth chattering with fear.

"G-G-GET THIS THING OFF M-M-ME!"

The three Bobs leaped over the sofa to help their mother. Together, they heaved on the snake's tail. But the snake was so **big** and **powerful** that it lifted the children high into the air!

# WHOOSH!

"ARGH!" they cried.

"If it's a puppy, then why does it keep *hissing?*" asked another Bob.

"He's only little. He hasn't learned to bark yet!" reasoned Silly Sid. "Come on, Fido. Give us a bark!"

"*HISS!*" hissed the snake, looking mightily confused.

"You called him Fido?" exclaimed Nancy. She couldn't believe her ears!

"Fido is a perfect name for a puppy!"

"For the last time, Fido is NOT A PUPPY!" she said. "Now, Silly Sid, for goodness' sake, help the children down. Then get this thing off me!"

One by one, Silly Sid plucked his Bobs off the snake as if they were apples from a tree. He set them down safely on the floor. Then he yanked hard on his pet's tail.

## TUG!

"*HISS!*" hissed the snake angrily as he unravelled at speed.

Poor Nancy was sent spinning.

"Come on, Fido," said Silly Sid, oblivious to the mayhem he'd just caused. "There's a good boy! Let's go for a nice walk!"

Then he put a dog collar round his pet's neck (hard to know where that is on a snake, as it all looks like neck), before attaching a lead. "Bob, Bob, Bob and Nancy! Me and Fido are off to the park! BYE!"

Taking his snake for a walk around the park was just one of the silly things Sid did with his new pet.

One Sunday afternoon, Silly Sid brought Fido to an old folks' home to visit his elderly mother. He thought the old people would love stroking the puppy.

*"HISS!"*

Oh my word! You've never seen old folk move so fast!

It is important to make sure your pet's teeth are clean, so Silly Sid brought Fido to the vet. However, when the vet tried to clean the snake's teeth, she very nearly lost an arm.

*"HISS!"*

**CHOMP!**
"HELP!"

At the end of every day, Silly Sid would give his pet a bath.

Pythons like being underwater, so it was always a struggle to get Fido out of the bath.

Every time Silly Sid tried, the snake would wrap himself round his master's arm and drag him in.

"AH!"

# SPLOOSH!

*"HISS! HISS! HISS!"*

Fido grew and grew until he was longer than a bus. One morning, Silly Sid shocked his wife and the Bobs with his silliest idea yet. He gathered them all in the living room to announce his news.

"Now, as Fido has been such a good puppy, I have decided to enter him for the greatest dog show on earth. **RUFFS!**"

Silly Sid's family burst out laughing.
"HA! HA! HA!"
"I have never heard anything so funny in my life!"

Fido stared at them, not liking the loud noise at all.

Nancy was absolutely tickled pink. "Oh! Silly Sid, you have out-sillied yourself this time! That is the silliest thing I have ever heard!"

"Why?" asked Silly Sid. Because he was so silly, he failed to see the funny side.

"BECAUSE FIDO'S A SNAKE!" his family chimed in together. "HA! HA! HA!"

"STOP BEING SO SILLY!" exclaimed Silly Sid. "Fido will win **RUFFS** and I will prove you all wrong!"

So Silly Sid had set himself an impossible task.
How on earth could a snake win a dog show?
As it turned out, with ease!
Please let me explain…
**RUFFS** is like a beauty pageant for dogs. Thousands of dogs from around the world take

part, and it is beamed into living rooms everywhere through the magic of television.

So Silly Sid put Fido back on the lead, which the snake loathed, and took him off to the huge hall where **RUFFS** was taking place.

The place was teaming with dogs, dogs and more dogs.

Amongst them were the dog superstars: **Mimi** the **Maltese**, who was handing out paw prints to her adoring fans… Abdul the Afghan hound, who was giving workshops on how best to blow-dry your hair… and, last but not least, there was *Polina* the *Pomeranian*.

Her fur was as white as snow, her ears were perfectly pointed up like little pink bows on top of her head and she had the *fluffiest* tail. No wonder Polina won **RUFFS** year after year. The Pomeranian was selling selfies with her for a thousand pounds a pop. If you didn't pay up fast enough in cash, Polina would bite you on the bottom. This was one wicked little dog.

# CHOMP!
"YEOW!"

So, into this cathedral of canines came a big scary snake.

As soon as Silly Sid brought Fido into the hall, there was chaos! It was

# POOCH PANDEMONIUM!

The dogs went barking mad. They went to flee. The owners didn't stand a chance. Their dogs yanked so hard on their leads that their owners were pulled to the ground.

*DOOF!*

Then they were dragged on their bellies down through the hall, into the streets and all the way home!

"STOP!"

Only one dog remained. The littlest, **yappiest, fiercest** dog: Polina.

**"YAP! YAP! YAP!"**

Fido slithered over to her, dragging Silly Sid all the way.

*WHOOSH!* The snake licked his lips.

"Come away now, Fido," ordered Silly Sid, tugging on the lead. Then, just as the snake was distracted for a moment by his master, Polina went on the **attack!**

**"YAP! YAP! YAP!"**

A bottom-biting expert, she raced round to the back of the snake. Struggling to find the snake's actual bottom, she bit hard on to the end of Fido's tail instead.

**CHOMP!**

So hard that the snake shot up into the air…
*WHOOSH!*

…and let out a hiss of pain!

"HHHIIISSSSSS!"

Fido bit on to a **RUFFS** sign that was hanging from the ceiling! Poor Silly Sid was dangling below, still holding tight to his pet's lead.

"HELP!" cried Silly Sid.

Polina took a running jump and leaped into the air.

She bit Silly Sid on the bottom. Not once, but twice!

**CHOMP! CHOMP!**

Once for each buttock.

"YEOW!" howled Silly Sid in pain.

This made Fido furious. Still holding on to the sign, the snake swung his tail down to the ground and hooked the little dog.

"YAP! YAP! YAP!" yapped Polina as she was lifted high into the air.

To get his revenge, Fido began spinning the little dog round and round.

WHIRR!

"LET GO, FIDO! THERE'S A GOOD DOG!" ordered Silly Sid.

"YAP! YAP! YAP!"

The faithful pet did just that. He let go of Polina mid spin and let her zoom through the air.

"YAP! YAP! YAP!"

Polina crashed through the roof.

SMASH!

She rocketed through the sky.

WHOOSH!

The Pomeranian was travelling so fast she landed in Pomerania!

With no dogs left in the hall, the **RUFFS** judges had to name a winner. Fearing they were going to have the life squeezed out of them if they didn't let the python win, Fido was named **BEST IN SHOW!**

"HISS!" hissed the snake in celebration, performing a little victory dance by bouncing around on his tail.

"YES!" exclaimed Silly Sid, who for once in his life had achieved something that was definitely **not** silly. He wrapped his arms round Fido, and together they twirled across the hall as if they were ballroom dancers!

# WHICH David Walliams

Once you've found out who you are, ask your friends and family who they are too!

Are you a child?

NO / YES

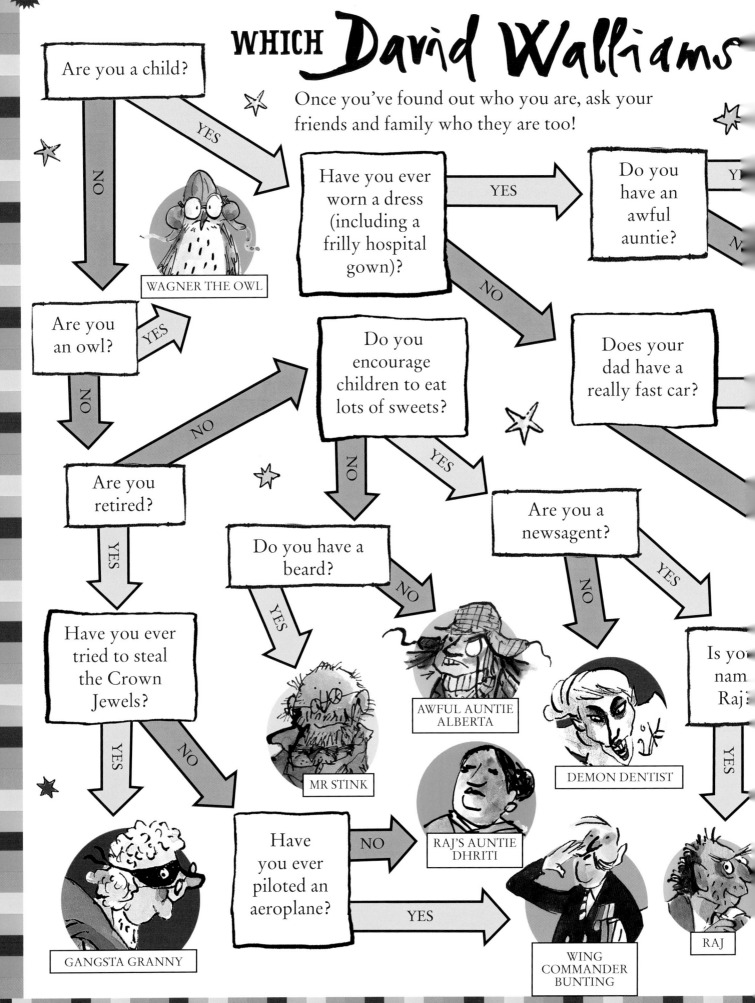

WAGNER THE OWL

Have you ever worn a dress (including a frilly hospital gown)?

YES / NO

Do you have an awful auntie?

Y / N

Are you an owl?

YES / NO

Are you retired?

YES / NO

Do you encourage children to eat lots of sweets?

NO / YES

Does your dad have a really fast car?

Have you ever tried to steal the Crown Jewels?

YES / NO

Do you have a beard?

YES / NO

Are you a newsagent?

NO / YES

AWFUL AUNTIE ALBERTA

MR STINK

DEMON DENTIST

RAJ'S AUNTIE DHRITI

Is yo nam Raj

YES

GANGSTA GRANNY

Have you ever piloted an aeroplane?

NO / YES

WING COMMANDER BUNTING

RAJ

# CHARACTER ARE *YOU*?

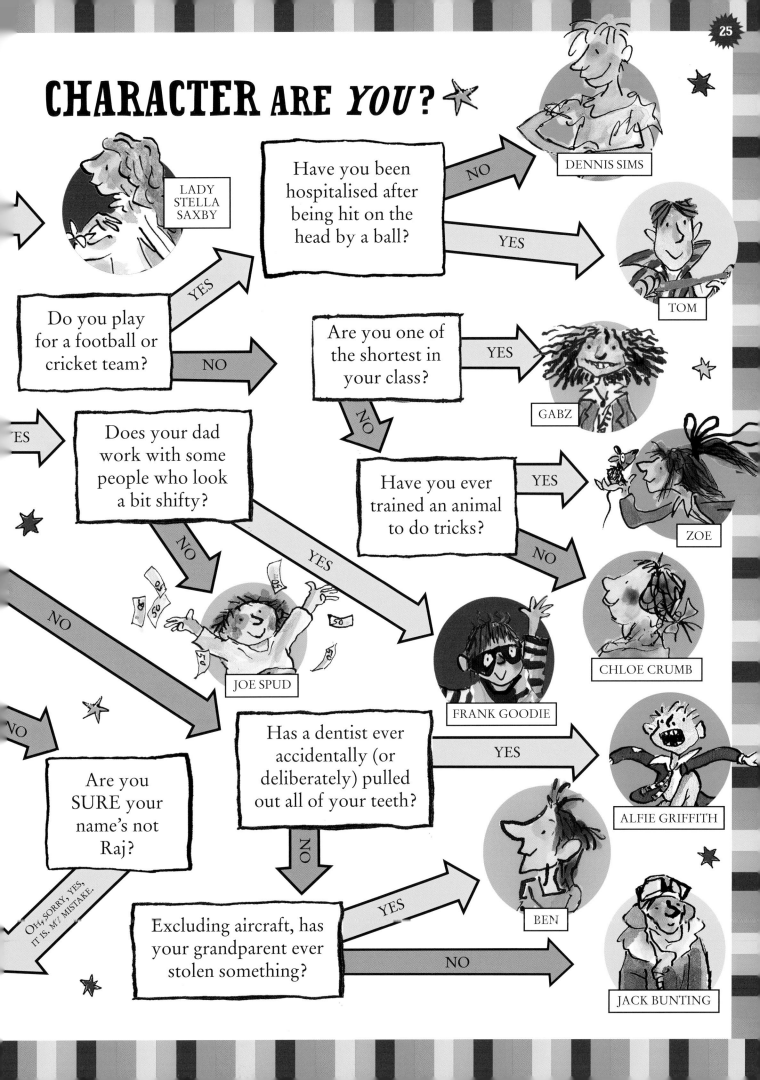

LADY STELLA SAXBY

**Have you been hospitalised after being hit on the head by a ball?**
— NO → DENNIS SIMS
— YES → TOM

**Do you play for a football or cricket team?**
— YES →
— NO →

**Are you one of the shortest in your class?**
— YES → GABZ
— NO →

**Have you ever trained an animal to do tricks?**
— YES → ZOE
— NO → CHLOE CRUMB

YES

**Does your dad work with some people who look a bit shifty?**
— NO →
— YES → JOE SPUD

NO

FRANK GOODIE

**Has a dentist ever accidentally (or deliberately) pulled out all of your teeth?**
— YES → ALFIE GRIFFITH
— NO →

NO

**Are you SURE your name's not Raj?**

*OH, SORRY, YES, IT IS. M? MISTAKE.*

**Excluding aircraft, has your grandparent ever stolen something?**
— YES → BEN
— NO → JACK BUNTING

# SLIME

# HOW TO MAKE SLIME

Welcome to the island of Mulch with its gruesome grown-ups who want to make children miserable. Is Ned brave enough to take them on with the power of slime?

## INGREDIENTS

 **BIG** dollop of PVA glue

 **1 TSP** of bicarbonate of soda

 **SQUIRT** of contact lens solution

 Food colouring

## INSTRUCTIONS

 Mix PVA glue and bicarbonate of soda

 Add food colouring to make your slime colourful and fun

 Add a squirt of contact lens solution and stir, and the slime will start to stick together

 Once it gets too sticky to stir, knead with your hands!

Roll up your sleeves and prepare to get messy! Bring on the slimepower…

Ask a grown-up to help you.

**MONSTROUS FACT**
The Island is owned by Aunt Greta Greed. In case you're wondering, she is the most appalling adult of all!

# SLIME

# SLIME SEARCH

The names of some unbearable inhabitants of Mulch (and some good ones, too!) are hidden in this grid. Cross them off as you go along.

| F | B | I | E | L | T | S | A | C | R | E | T | T | I | L | Y | T | T | I | K |
| C | U | E | X | M | Y | H | F | Z | S | N | T | L | W | M | Q | E | T | M | D |
| G | K | D | L | G | L | E | N | D | A | G | L | U | T | T | O | N | T | A | O |
| I | T | M | O | J | M | K | S | E | T | I | U | W | B | A | X | I | A | D | U |
| G | R | U | T | W | A | G | C | N | D | V | H | Z | F | L | R | D | N | A | I |
| A | L | N | E | I | E | C | R | D | R | T | C | V | H | M | E | C | K | M | P |
| N | V | D | N | B | D | W | O | V | A | U | X | L | Y | E | W | Y | N | E | D |
| T | O | E | T | U | A | D | S | R | H | Q | B | E | R | D | H | E | L | S | O |
| I | E | N | K | Z | L | D | L | E | M | T | S | G | R | M | I | D | R | I | H |
| C | S | V | E | F | B | H | S | E | I | L | A | I | M | O | D | I | B | L | J |
| T | W | Y | M | Y | M | X | U | V | S | T | Z | O | Q | N | I | R | U | E | W |
| I | I | C | G | R | S | L | I | M | E | U | J | I | A | D | E | P | T | N | F |
| D | U | X | S | P | H | B | D | R | X | T | R | N | H | E | S | N | V | Z | R |
| D | N | O | T | T | U | L | G | N | E | L | G | H | D | N | Z | I | T | I | G |
| L | T | E | C | Y | W | T | Y | I | M | E | W | F | B | V | O | A | N | O | S |
| E | R | S | H | M | N | Q | K | H | V | A | E | C | M | Y | S | T | W | S | I |
| S | A | O | P | U | R | G | L | V | S | P | G | R | X | U | E | P | J | L | C |
| M | O | C | A | D | E | T | J | E | M | I | M | A | Q | I | C | A | H | O | M |
| H | J | V | E | I | T | O | T | S | A | W | A | F | L | D | G | C | X | T | K |
| A | U | H | C | L | U | M | U | A | C | R | T | R | O | A | S | T | L | H | D |

- AUNT GRETA GREED
- EDMOND ENVY
- GLEN GLUTTON
- SLIME
- NED
- JEMIMA
- MADAME SILENZIO SLOTH
- EDMUND ENVY
- GLENDA GLUTTON
- MULCH
- TIDDLES
- GIGANTIC TIDDLES
- KITTY LITTER CASTLE
- CAPTAIN PRIDE

ANSWERS ON PAGE 70

# ALL ABOUT THE WORLD'S WORST MONSTERS

**WARNING:** This book is bursting with ogres, ghosts, aliens, zombies… and more!

Here are some of the marvellous monsters and other fabulous faces you will meet in these stories.

## WHAT'S IT ABOUT?

This spooktacular collection of 10 terrifying tales features mythical creatures of just about every kind.

### LORD PHANTOM

Meet the cold-tomato-soup-loving ghost, Lord Phantom. After a five-hundred-year slumber, this see-through chap wakes up in a theme park where his home once was.

### WOLFY

There was never a furrier little boy. In fact, Wolfy's whole family are furry. Even their car is furry! Lots of people are afraid of Wolfy, but will his new pen pal change all of that?

### BYRON

What happens when a teddy goes all skew-whiff? Byron, that's what! He's not your average soft toy. His arms and legs are all higgledy-piggledy, plus his fur is distinctly stinky.

### AMBER

Meet Amber. There is nothing out of the ordinary about this little girl. Apart from, of course, that her family are likely to be vampires. Well, Amber is pretty sure that they are!

### ROSE

She's about to uncover the truth about the Loch Ness Monster.

## ARTHUR
Down in the cellar of Baskerville School Arthur discovers his headmaster turned into a statue. Luckily Arthur is the school detective, and his bag is stuffed with everything needed to solve a mystery.

## JESS
Whenever Jess spends time with her mummy (a LOT!), adventure follows. Jess's mummy is the loveliest, clumsiest mummy around. So, what could go wrong on a visit to the Egyptian mummies?

## THE ABOMINABLE
### BUT NICE SNOWMAN
When explorer Lord Blunderbuss hears about an "Abominable Snowman" he grabs his rifle in a flash, keen to add it to his stuffed animal collection. It's time for this icy beast to prove they're a Rather Nice Snowman.

Draw your monstrous creation in the box and write a few lines to describe its features below.

# THE WORLD'S WORST MONSTERS

# MUMMY THE MUMMY

**DARE YOU ENTER THE WORLD OF MONSTERS?** Read on for a fiercely funny story featuring a terrifying tale of marvellous mummies!

When is a mummy not a mummy? When the mummy is, in fact, a mummy.

Let's begin this **HORROR** story with a history lesson.

This is a mummy...

...an Ancient Egyptian who, after death, had been mummified to prepare them for the afterlife.

The priests of the time would remove all the insides except the heart, embalm the body to preserve it, then wrap it in strips of linen until it was completely covered.

These mummies were discovered thousands of years later, in tombs buried deep under the sand in the deserts of Egypt. Legend has it that disturbing these burial sites causes ancient curses to be unleashed. Some even believed that if you unearthed these mummies they came back to life as monsters!

Now, this is also a mummy.

This is Jess's mummy. Jess is a little girl in glasses who loves her mummy, even though she is the clumsiest person on earth. Mummy was a one-woman disaster zone: Stepping inside the house from a rainstorm, Mummy closed her umbrella on her head. She couldn't see a thing.

Repairing a vase that she had broken, Mummy managed to superglue her dress to the table.

**GLOOP!**

And when she stood up and walked away, the dress stayed stuck. Mummy stood there in her undercrackers.

Leaning over the safety barrier too far at the zoo, Mummy plunged into the penguin pool. The poor lady couldn't hoist herself out of the water. Mummy ended up splashing around in there for the best part of a year, surviving only on a diet of raw fish.

Her daughter Jess couldn't be more different from her. She was a shy, studious girl who had been learning about Ancient Egypt in school. Everything about the subject electrified her.

However, what fascinated Jess most were the mummies. She imagined them coming back to life to wreak revenge on those who had disturbed their final resting place, and she longed to see one in real life.

So, on the eve of her **birthday**, Jess pleaded, "Mummy, please can you take me to the British Museum for my **birthday** so I can see the mummies with my own eyes?"

"Darling, please, no! Those things give Mummy the willies!" replied her mother, putting down her book, which was upside down.

"Please?"

"No! Can't we go to the waterslides instead?"

Jess couldn't believe her ears. "Mummy, you have a lifetime ban from the waterslides! You tried to go up them rather than down them!"

"All I did was break every bone in my body. A lot of fuss about nothing, if you ask me!"

"HUMPH!" huffed Jess. "It's my birthday and I want to go to the British Museum. But you must promise me, Mummy, to be on your absolute best behaviour. No more disasters!"

"I PROMISE!" replied Mummy with a big, broad smile.

So, the very next morning, mother and daughter set off on the train. Jess was sure that a trip to the British Museum was going to make today the best **birthday** ever.

As soon as the pair arrived, Mummy announced she needed the loo.

"I'll be in the mummy room," said Jess, as Mummy scuttled off.

Stepping into the room, Jess was struck silent with awe. All around were ORNATE coffins, each one containing an Ancient Egyptian mummy.

Now, Mummy had a bad habit of using up all the toilet paper at home because she always tugged too hard on the end of the roll, and the entire thing would *unspool*.

This is precisely what she did now.

Mummy yanked on the end and the bumper-size roll began *unspooling* at speed.

In her futile attempts to roll the paper back into place, Mummy managed to tangle herself up in it. Soon she was covered from head to toe in toilet paper. Mummy now looked exactly like a mummy! As she stumbled out of the cubicle with her arms outstretched, the ladies at the basins screamed in horror.

Mummy the mummy tried to speak, but her words were **muffled** by the toilet paper stuck in her mouth. All you could hear were scary-sounding moans.

**"URGH!"**

Mummy's eyes were completely covered so she couldn't see where she was going.

And now she was **LUMBERING** along the corridor of the museum in the direction of the mummy room.

Jess was completely immersed in the ancient world of wonder when the bandaged figure **shuffled** into the room behind her. As all the other visitors ran off, she felt a tap on her shoulder. She turned round slowly to see this mummy – well, her mummy – behind her.

"ARGH!" screamed the girl. "It's true! There is a curse!"

Jess picked up the nearest weapon she could find, a leaflet on Ancient Egypt, and she tried to poke the mummy with it, but all that happened was that the paper bent.

Then she had a better idea. Jess grabbed hold of the end of what she assumed was linen (but was of course bog roll) and yanked hard.

In an instant, Mummy the mummy began *spinning* wildly.

As the toilet paper *t w i rl e d* off, she whirled around the room, COLLIDING with the ancient coffins which, one by one, toppled off their plinths and crashed to the ground.

Even the little coffin containing the mummified cat broke.

**SMISH!**

Now all the mummies had been well and truly woken from their eternal sleeps. The mummified cat also began to stir.

With the roll of toilet paper now unfurled on the museum floor, Mummy was finally free.

"MUMMY!" exclaimed Jess. "I thought you were a real mummy come to life!"

Jess rushed over to Mummy and gave her the biggest hug.

"Oh! I am so relieved!" she sighed.

What Mummy could see, but her daughter could not, was that the real mummies lying on the floor were twitching into life.

"Erm, Jessica…"

Jess spun round. A dozen ancient mummies were rising to their feet and stumbling towards them with their hands outstretched. Even the mummified cat was approaching.

"*HISS!*"

The mummies began trying to grab at the pair. From under the bandages, their eyes shone **red** like demons.

"NO!" screamed Jess as a mummified hand gripped on to her arm. "GET OFF ME!"

"What shall we do?" cried Mummy.

"I KNOW!" cried Jess. "Grab one end of the toilet roll, and I will grab the other!"

"Then what?" said Mummy.

"Wrap them all up in it!"

The pair each took an end of the roll and ran around the museum in huge circles, wrapping the mummies in paper so they couldn't come any closer.

The mummified cat was clever, though, and it ducked out of the way and hid behind a statue.

Meanwhile, the mummies were bound up together. They couldn't move a millimetre.

At that moment, Mummy took her daughter's hand and they slunk out of the museum, not even stopping at the gift shop.

It was only when Jess was being tucked into bed that night that she remembered something.

"The mummified cat! It came back to life, but we didn't wrap it in toilet roll!"

"I am sure the security guards have found it."

"I do hope so," replied Jess.

"So, Jessica, did you have a lovely birthday?"

"Well, apart from you being wrapped head to toe in a roll of toilet paper, destroying most of the precious artefacts in the museum and bringing some Ancient Egyptian mummies back to life, yes!"

Mummy smiled. She bent down to kiss her daughter on the head, but slipped on Jess's slipper and fell on top of her instead.

"I am so sorry, darling!"

"Don't worry, Mummy. I love you! And I always will!"

"I love you too! Sweet dreams, my beautiful angel!"

As Mummy closed the door, she trapped her nightdress inside...

R I P !

...ripping the whole thing off.

"Not again!" came a voice from the other side of the door. "I'm all in the nudey nudes!"

Her daughter couldn't help but burst into laughter.

"HA! HA! HA!"

She felt so lucky having the funniest mummy in the world. Tired, Jess rolled over on to her side to sleep. Just then, she heard a gentle tapping on the window.

Jess slid out of bed and tiptoed over to investigate. Peeping through the gap in the curtains, she could see something perched on the ledge.

It was the mummified cat from the museum, its eyes glowing red like a demon. This was no nightmare!

This was really happening!

"HISS!"

# GANGSTA GRANNY

# HOW TO BLING YOUR GRANNY'S RIDE

IS YOUR GRANNY A GANGSTA? DOES YOUR GRANNY HAVE A MOBILITY SCOOTER THAT NEEDS JAZZING UP? HERE ARE SOME TIPS ON HOW TO MAKE HER SCOOTER A SUPER-DUPER SCOOTER...

In-basket sound system (plays hymns at 1,000 decibels)

Motorbike handlebars

Framed photo of King Charles in his swimming trunks

GET SOME PLAIN WHITE PAPER AND DRAW YOUR OWN IDEAS!

Souped-up lawnmower engine (max speed 12 mph)

Retractable knitting needles in wheels (for taking out other scooters in the post-office queue)

# FING

# COLOUR IN THAT FING

Along their journey, Mr and Mrs Meek come across The *Monsterpedia*. This book is filled with weird and wacky monsters, such as Fing, Dumdum, Eebinkibonk and Crunkletoad.

Use your pens or pencils to give them colour!

FING

## ALL ABOUT FING

Myrtle Meek always gets her mitts on everything she wants and more. So when she asks her parents for a FING, they will stop at nothing to get hold of one for her. The only problem is, they have no idea what a FING is…

CRUNKLETOAD

EEBINKIBONK

AAGADONGDONG

DUMDUM

BOOBOO

CREATE YOUR OWN MONSTER!

# AWFUL AUNTIE
## AUNTIE ALBERTA'S
# OWLEUM

Here are the plans for Auntie Alberta's Owl Museum, or "Owleum". Inside, you will find various incredibly rare breeds of owl immortalised forever.

CHAMELEON OWL: ABLE TO DISGUISE ITSELF TO BLEND IN TO ANY SITUATION

THE VERY-SMALL-WINGED OWL: NESTS HIGH UP ON CLIFFS; LIFE EXPECTANCY OF EIGHT SECONDS

AUSTRALIAN OWL

RICHARD OWL: NOT AN OWL, BUT A MAN WHOSE SURNAME HAPPENED TO BE OWL

A COLLECTION OF RARE STUFFED OWLS

UNDERWATER OWL

TYRANNOROWLUS REX: THE EARLIEST-KNOWN OWL

ENTRANCE

KNIGHT OWL

PUFFER OWL: INFLATES TO THE SIZE OF A BEACH BALL WHEN THREATENED

LESSER-SPOTTED OWL

SPOTTED OWL

TRANSYLVANIAN VAMPIRE OWL: ONLY COMES OUT IN THE DAYTIME

MOON OWL: ONLY FOUND IN THE CRATERS OF THE EARTH'S MOON

MICRO OWL: THE WORLD'S SMALLEST OWL, AT ONLY 1MM TALL

BARN OWL: NAMED AFTER ITS DISTINCTIVE BARN SHAPE

MERM-OWL: HALF OWL, HALF FISH

JET-PROPELLED OWL: THIS OWL FLIES SOLELY BY USING THE POWER OF ITS OWN TRUMPS

## BABY-OWL EXPERIENCE:
### YOU DRESS UP AS A BABY OWL AND A CLOCKWORK MOTHER OWL FEEDS YOU REGURGITATED WORMS AND MOUSE HEADS

## OWLEUM GIFT SHOP,
### WHERE YOU CAN BUY ITEMS INCLUDING. . .

- Tea Towl – an owl whose feathers you can use to dry the dishes
- Beach Towl – a larger owl whose feathers you can use to dry yourself on the beach
- Stuff-your-own-owl kit (owl not included)
- Guess Whoo? – the owl board game
- Scented pencil toppers (smells of owl droppings)
- "World's Best Owl" mug – a fun gift for your nearest and dearest owl
- Model Owleum – a perfect miniature replica of the Owleum (it's so accurate that it even has a tiny gift shop inside with an even smaller model Owleum in, and so on).
- Owl sandals – ideal for when you take your owl to the beach
- A 101 Relaxing Owl Screeches CD
- Owl repellent – for people who don't like owls
- Owl wings – fly like an owl!* (* Not suitable for flying)

## THE WAGNER EXHIBITION

A room dedicated to the memory of my favourite owl, Wagner.

OIL PAINTINGS I PAINTED OF WAGNER AS SOME OF MY FAVOURITE HISTORICAL CHARACTERS

BOUDICCA, BRITON WHO BATTLED THE ROMANS

ENGLAND'S MOST FAMOUS KING, KING HENRY VIII

RASPUTIN, THE MAD MONK OF RUSSIA

EXIT

# CODE NAME BANANAS

# ALL ABOUT CODE NAME BANANAS

This epic story about a super-smart boy and his unusual BFF (big furry friend) is jam-packed with adventure! Just take a look…

## What's the peel?

It's 1940 and Britain is at war with Germany. Orphan boy Eric spends most of his days at London Zoo where he meets Gertrude, a remarkable gorilla. When bombs start falling all over the city, Eric must rescue Gertrude, with a little help from his zookeeper uncle.

### Eric

Eric is 11 years old. He is short and shy and lost both of his parents in the war. His friendship with Gertrude is the best thing in his life.

### Gertrude

Gertrude is the star attraction at London Zoo. She loves bananas, putting on a show and Eric.

### Uncle Sid

Sid is Eric's great-uncle. He lost his legs in the First World War and would give anything to prove himself to be a hero.

## CODE NAME BANANAS

# GERTRUDE'S PARTY TRICKS

When it comes to party tricks, Gertrude is your gal. Here are a few of her favourites!

PEELING A BANANA WITH HER FEET

WAGGLING HER BOTTOM

STICKING OUT HER TONGUE

PERFORMING A CARTWHEEL

What's YOUR best party trick? Draw or write them here.

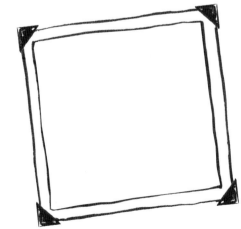

# ALL ABOUT THE WORLD'S WORST CHILDREN

## What's it about?

Across the series, you will be lucky enough to meet more than 30 delightfully dreadful girls and boys – each has their own terrible tale to tell.

If you are feeling particularly daring, then it's time to meet a few of the hilariously horrible gang from books 1, 2 and 3.

### Sofia Sofa

This is the gal who loves TV so much that she's at risk of transforming into a sofa!

### Dribbling Drew

Drew's drool is out of control, and it winds up getting him into all kinds of trouble.

### Blubbering Bertha

When she's not too busy sobbing, this bawling big sister loves nothing more than telling tales.

### Windy Mindy

Mindy has a unique talent for breaking wind. She can even play a tune on the tuba with her bottom!

# Humbert the Hungry Baby

Let's not forget the hungriest baby in town, Humbert. This big bubba eats anything and everything.

# Cruel Clarissa

She may talk sweetly, wearing her adorable dresses and cutesy bows but... do not be fooled by Clarissa!

# No No Noe

"No" is the only word you will hear when Noe's around. She loves it so much, especially when it annoys everyone else.

# Hank's Pranks

Who remembers Hank and his endless pranks? His poor, poor family often get the brunt of his tricks.

# Tandy's Tantrums

When it comes to tantrums, Tandy's are titanic! Her ear-splitting shrieks go on all day long.

# Boastful Barnabus

Barnabus is the most braggy, big-headed kid around. He even cast himself as every character in the school play!

# MEET THE BLUNDERS

You can count on the Blunders to make a real mess of things! This family of upper-class twits will have you laughing out loud with their antics.

## WHAT'S IT ABOUT?

When the Blunder family home, Blunder Hall, is threatened by the man from the bank, they must come together to save it. With a name like the Blunders, what could happen next?

OLD LADY BLUNDER

LOVES SHOOTING THINGS

OBSESSED WITH HORSES

BERTIE

BETSY

INVENTOR OF THE UNI-SHOE AND 5,268TH IN LINE FOR THE THRONE

## ALSO FEATURING...

- Butler: the butler
- Cedric: the pet ostrich
- Pegasus: Lady Blunder's imaginary horse
- Tiddlypops: a ghost cat
- Bottom burps
- Life-sized board games
- A knicker circus

BUNNY

BRUTUS

A NIGHTMARE!

ABSOLUTELY FILTHY

# UN-BLUNDER
## THESE BLUNDERS

The Blunders have made some blunders with the words below. Can you unscramble them to find the correct spellings?

WRITE YOUR ANSWERS IN THESE BOXES

HINT!
You can find all these words on the opposite page.

SOTRCHI

YNUNB

USSEGAP

DLUBNER

"IF ONLY THERE WAS AN INVENTION FOR SUCH A TASK..."

SIRCUC

TUBREL

# THE BLUNDERS

# COLOUR IN
# THE BLUNDERS

Grab your pens or pencils to colour the Blunders in the bath!

Can you guess what's happening here?

# INVENTIONS WITH BERTIE

Bertie has invented many… interesting things over the years. Can you match the names of these inventions to the items in the picture, and then colour each one?

**a** Roller-skates for cats

**b** Bomb-proof nappies

**c** Rope on a soap

**d** Mashed-potato blaster

**e** Bubble-free bubble bath

**f** The supersucker

**g** Fur in a can

**h** Edible socks

**ANSWERS ON PAGE 70**

# ALL ABOUT ASTROCHIMP

What do you get when you cross a chimp with a spacecraft? A load of monkey business, that's what!

## WHAT'S IT ABOUT?

Chump the chimp isn't your average chimpanzee. He's the first chimp, specially selected by NASA, to go into outer space. That's right, SPACE! A chimp and a spacecraft. What could possibly go wrong?

## MEET CHUMP

Chump the chimp grew up in Central Park Zoo before being selected for his special mission. He's very silly and loves bananas.

One small step for Chump… one giant mistake for humankind.

**BARDOT THE COOL CAT** – the world's first catstronaut.

**DMITRI THE ROGUE** – the first dog space pirate.

**THE QUEEN OF THE GIANT FRUIT FLIES** – she lives for revenge (and fruit)!

**CHOTI THE GERBIL** – nothing is known about her. She is a complete mystery!

**TING AND HONG THE DO-GOODERS** – the slowest rescue team in the universe.

# ASTROCHIMP

# THE WORLD OF ASTROCHIMP

## (THE TRUE FACTS)

All the characters in *Astrochimp* are based on the real animals that were blasted into space.

**1947:** The US sent fruit flies into space on a V-2 rocket.

**1949:** The US sent a rhesus macaque monkey named Albert II into space on another V-2 rocket.

**1957:** Russia sent a dog named Laika on Sputnik 2 to orbit the Earth.

**1959:** The US sent a rhesus macaque named Miss Able and a squirrel monkey named Miss Baker into space on a Jupiter rocket.

**1961:** Ham became the first great ape in space. He was even given some responsibility in piloting his Mercury spacecraft. He survived and became a national hero – even inspiring this little-known book called *Astrochimp*!

**1963:** France sent a cat named Félicette into space on a Veronique rocket.

**1967:** Argentina launched a rat named Belisario into space on a Yarará rocket.

**1968:** Russia sent up two tortoises on Zond 5 in 1968.

**1973:** The US sent cross spiders named Anita and Arabella into space with astronauts on the rocket Skylab 3.

**2007:** And in case you were thinking that gerbils were never blasted into space, they were! Russia sent them up in 2007!

# ASTRO CHIMP

# KERUNCH!

## Metal struck metal!

Chump's capsule had been rammed by a **huge** spaceship. A pirate's skull-and-crossbones flag flew on top of it.

THE HOUND OF HORROR

The ship locked on to the open emergency escape hatch of Chump's capsule.

Instantly, the ice-cold capsule was flooded with warm air.

FOOSH!

The deep-frozen chimp* began to thaw.

Now Chump's ice-encrusted eyes opened for the first time in half a century!

An upside-down dog's head sporting an eye patch poked through the hatch. The dog barked in a Russian accent.

HAND OVER YOUR BANANAS OR DEATH AWAITS YOU!

*You will be glad to know you can't find deep-frozen chimps next to the deep-frozen peas in the supermarket.

Dmitri was a stray who had been found living rough on the mean backstreets of Moscow. Years before Chump's mission, he was selected to make history as the first animal in space.

The Russian space programme chose a stray dog, as it would be more able to endure the cold and hunger up in space.

Dmitri was strapped into his spacecraft and blasted up into space. His mission was a success: he survived!

But little did HE know that there was no plan to bring him back to Earth. He was left alone in his craft, floating across the universe. He had ZERO CHANCE OF SURVIVAL.

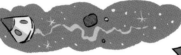

But the dog was dogged. Dmitri was determined to survive by becoming the first DOG SPACE PIRATE! That's why he was demanding Chump's bananas!

Can we discuss this? I am rather fond of bananas.

Are you NUTS?

No. I am a chimpanzee.

Hand over all your bananas! Now!

NO!

Right! That's it! I am coming in to get them!

With that, he slid down into the capsule.

Leave me and my bananas alone!

HA! HA! NEVER!

Feeling as if he were going to lose his bananas and his life, Chump searched for something to throw at the dog.

He reached into the tiny hatch marked EMERGENCY BANANAS.

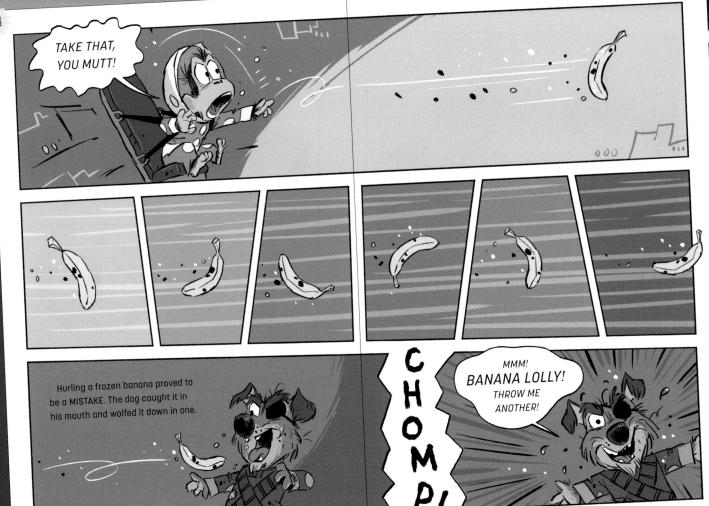

# ALL ABOUT SPACEBOY

UFOs, aliens, government secrets, and a mysterious boy in a silver spacesuit… *Spaceboy* is out of this world!

## What's it about?

12-year-old Ruth is OBSESSED with space. It's all she can think about, so you can imagine her excitement when a real-life UFO crash-lands in a cornfield near her home. Suddenly it's bye-bye awful auntie and hello supersonic adventure!

## Ruth

Ruth is an orphan who lives with her awful auntie in a farmhouse in the back of beyond. She loves outer space and her pet dog Yuri.

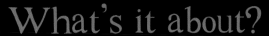

## Aunt Dorothy

Aunt Dorothy is – you guessed it – Ruth's aunt. After taking Ruth in, she put her straight to work on the farm.

## Yuri

Yuri is a stray that Ruth adopted. He is named after the pilot, Yuri Gagarin, who was the first human ever to venture into outer space.

## Spaceboy

Spaceboy is quite the mystery. He wears a shiny silver spacesuit and speaks in a spooky voice.

### SPACE RACE, WHAT?

This book is set in the 1960s when the world was gripped by the space race. This was a time of competition between the USA and Russia over who could conquer space exploration first.

# SPACEBOY

# MAKE YOUR OWN SPACESUIT

Listen up, space cadets! If you want to be an astronaut like Spaceboy, you'll need a spacesuit. Here's how to make your very own – the safe way.

Spaceboy was on to something with this design. Let's use it as inspiration!

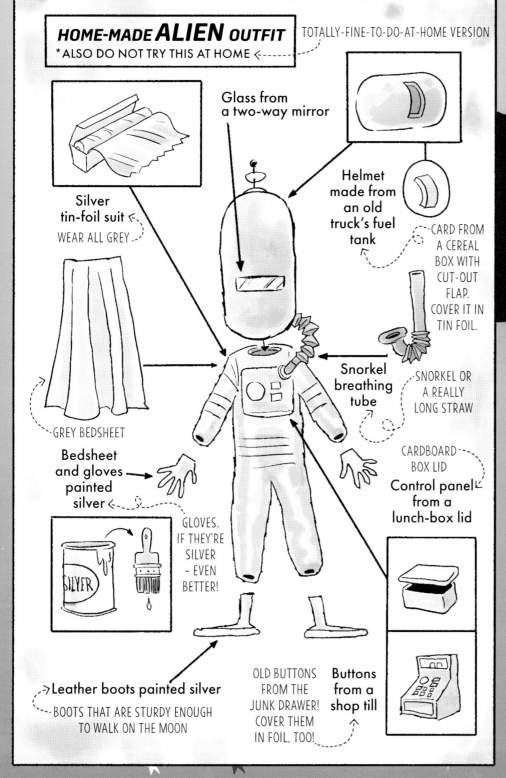

**HOME-MADE ALIEN OUTFIT**
\*ALSO DO NOT TRY THIS AT HOME ←

TOTALLY-FINE-TO-DO-AT-HOME VERSION

Glass from a two-way mirror

Silver tin-foil suit ←
WEAR ALL GREY

Helmet made from an old truck's fuel tank

CARD FROM A CEREAL BOX WITH CUT-OUT FLAP. COVER IT IN TIN FOIL.

Snorkel breathing tube

SNORKEL OR A REALLY LONG STRAW

GREY BEDSHEET

Bedsheet and gloves painted silver ←

GLOVES. IF THEY'RE SILVER – EVEN BETTER!

SILVER

CARDBOARD BOX LID

Control panel from a lunch-box lid

Leather boots painted silver
BOOTS THAT ARE STURDY ENOUGH TO WALK ON THE MOON

OLD BUTTONS FROM THE JUNK DRAWER! COVER THEM IN FOIL, TOO!

Buttons from a shop till

**NOT PICTURED BUT ALSO NEEDED:**

★ Tape (lots of it) to stick stuff together.

★ Ribbon or string to tie the helmet in place.

★ Scissors, and a parent or guardian to help with the boring task of cutting things up.

# SPACEBOY

# CONSTELLATION STAR-TO-STAR

Can you connect the dots in this constellation from another planet? What will you find?

⭐ **START**

What can Ruth see through her telescope this time?

# BILLIONAIRE BOY

## A LOO-ROLL ROLLING PIN*
### LOO ROLLS REQUIRED: 3

INSTRUCTIONS: Just stick three loo rolls together in a row. That's it. This is the perfect loo-roll model to make if you're a beginner.
* Do not try to roll food with this as it will make the food smell of toilets.

Joe Spud's prized possession is a loo-roll rocket made by his dad, Leonard Spud.

## A LOO-ROLL RACING CAR
### LOO ROLLS REQUIRED: 8

INSTRUCTIONS: Use loo rolls for the wheels, but for the chassis... also use loo rolls. Loo-roll engine optional. To capture the feel of a real Formula One race, every half an hour hurriedly yank off the loo-roll wheels from your loo-roll racing car, then speedily replace them with four fresh new loo rolls, ideally in under 3.7 seconds.

## A LOO-ROLL FORT AND LOO-ROLL SOLDIERS
### LOO ROLLS REQUIRED: 48 IN TOTAL – 36 (FORT) 12 (SOLDIERS)

INSTRUCTIONS: Use loo rolls to build the outer walls, then, for the turrets, use loo rolls. However, this is where things take a turn, so pay close attention. For the soldiers, use loo rolls that you've painted. To make your loo-roll fort like a real fort, pour water round it to create a moat. (Please note: unlike a real fort, this will make your loo-roll fort go soggy.)

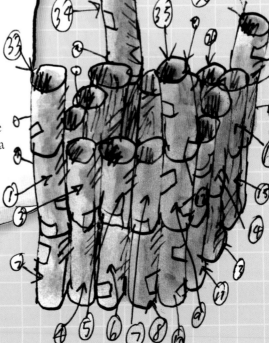

## A LOO-ROLL TELESCOPE
### LOO ROLLS REQUIRED: 4

INSTRUCTIONS: To the untrained eye, this might look very similar to the loo-roll rolling pin. But, to an expert loo-roll modeller, it's markedly different because instead of using THREE loo rolls, this model uses FOUR, which is 33.3% more loo rolls. Never ever try to use your loo-roll telescope as a loo-roll rolling pin as this may have disastrous, possibly even fatal, consequences.

## A LOO-ROLL SPACE ROCKET
### LOO ROLLS REQUIRED: 7

INSTRUCTIONS: Use four loo rolls for the rocket base. But to make the shaft of the rocket I am using a very specialist building material – loo rolls. It is actually possible to launch this loo-roll rocket into space. All you need to do is attach it to a real NASA rocket with Blu-tack. If you don't live near the Kennedy Space Center in Florida (or you do, but don't have any spare Blu-tack), just ask a grown-up with a very strong arm to throw it as high as they can.

## A LOO-ROLL LOO
### LOO ROLLS REQUIRED: 426

INSTRUCTIONS: I think the picture is pretty self-explanatory. Just stick the loo rolls together until they look like that.
WARNING: Do not try to use this loo-roll loo as a loo. It is not plumbed in, so anything that is splashed or plopped into it will totally ruin the cardboard. I found that out the hard way.

# GANGSTA GRANNY

# FIND THE BLACK CAT

There are a lot of characters in the image below, but only one black cat! Can you spot where the black cat is hiding?

ANSWER ON PAGE 70

# GANGSTA GRANNY

# SHINY SPOT THE DIFFERENCE

To be a good thief you need a quick hand and a sharp eye. Let's see how good yours are. Can you spot the 10 differences between these pictures?

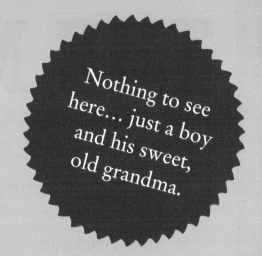

Nothing to see here... just a boy and his sweet, old grandma.

a

b

ANSWERS ON PAGE 70

# THE MEGA QUIZ!

You've made it to the end of the book, now let's see how much you can remember. It's time for… THE MEGA QUIZ!

*Think long and hard about your answers, you wouldn't want to disappoint The World's Worst Teachers…*

1. What's the name of Ruth's awful auntie in *Spaceboy*?
   a. Aunt Adelaide
   b. Aunt Dora
   c. Aunt Dorothy

2. In which book will you find the city of Bedlam?
   a. *Spaceboy*
   b. *Robodog*
   c. *The Blunders*

3. What's the name of the school in *Megamonster*?
   a. The Cruel School
   b. The Drool School
   c. The Ghoul School

4. What type of toy is Byron in *The World's Worst Monsters*?
   a. Teddy bear
   b. Wolf
   c. Robot

5. In *The World's Worst Children*, Sofia might turn into a…
   a. Bed
   b. Pair of shoes
   c. Sofa

6. What does Amber, the leader of
    *The Midnight Gang*, dream
    of becoming one day?
    a. A composer
    b. A world-famous explorer
    c. A superhero

You especially don't want to get on the wrong side of Miss Seethe. That ghastly woman loves giving out detentions!

7. What is the name of the Blunders' butler?
    a. Butler
    b. Cedric
    c. Brutus

8. What does Gangsta Granny like to collect?
    a. Coins
    b. Stamps
    c. Jewellery

9. Which World's Worst Pet has
    a terrible temper?
    a. Furp the fish
    b. Silly Sid's snake Fido
    c. Griselda the grizzly bear

10. How old is the so-called
    Ice Monster in the
    newspaper Elsie steals?
    a. 1,000 years old
    b. 10,000 years old
    c. 1000,000 years old

11. What is the name of the greedy girl
    who wants a Fing?
    a. Myrtle Meek
    b. Susie Snide
    c. Lucy Lavish

12. What year is *Code Name Bananas* set?
    a. 1930
    b. 1940
    c. 1950

13. In which book will you find the island of Mulch?
    a. *Slime*
    b. *Fing*
    c. *Megamonster*

14. Who is Ruth's dog Yuri named after in *Spaceboy*?
    a. The first animal to go into outer space
    b. The person who invented the rocket
    c. The first human to go into outer space

15. What position is Bertie Blunder in line for
    the throne?
    a. 5,268th
    b. 4,379th
    c. 6,468th

16. Fill in the missing word: Bumble the … budgie
    a. Babbling
    b. Burgling
    c. Bragging

ANSWERS ON PAGE 70

17. What makes Amber special in
*The World's Worst Monsters*?
    a. Her family might be vampires
    b. She is a ghost
    c. Her family are werewolves

18. Who is NOT a member of the Police Dog
School in *Robodog*?
    a. Scarper
    b. Plank
    c. Growler

19. What is the name of Gangsta Granny's grandson?
    a. Jack
    b. Ben
    c. Sam

20. How did Tom end up in Lord Funt hospital
in *The Midnight Gang*?
    a. He was hit on the head with a cricket ball
    b. He broke his arm falling off monkey bars
    c. He got tonsillitis

# ANSWERS

Page 8

1. *RATBURGER* AND *BAD DAD*
2. THE NATIONAL TROUSER MUSEUM – ALTHOUGH IT DOES SOUND EXCELLENT
3. A BILLION POUNDS – JOE SPUD FROM *BILLIONAIRE BOY*
4. GILBERT GOODIE FROM *BAD DAD*
5. BEN'S FROM *GANGSTA GRANNY*
6. THE MIDNIGHT GANG
7. MR STINK
8. ZOE FROM *RATBURGER*
9. ST AGATHA'S SCHOOL FOR ARISTOCRATIC GIRLS
10. FIND HIM YOURSELF... ONLY JOKING. HE IS BEHIND THE TREE OPPOSITE THE CRUMBS' RESIDENCE

Page 10

Page 27

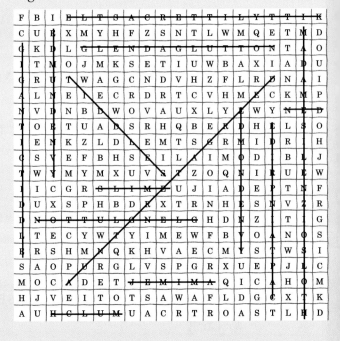

Page 14

Page 15

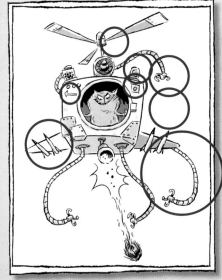